Alice Walker's

The Color Purple

BookCaps Study Guide

www.bookcaps.com

© 2011. All Rights Reserved.

Table of Contents

HISTORICAL CONTEXT 3

PLOT 5

CHARACTERS 7

THEMES 15

CHAPTER SUMMARIES 21

    LETTERS 1-10 22
    LETTERS 11-20 26
    LETTERS 21-30 29
    LETTERS 31-40 33
    LETTERS 41-50 36
    LETTERS 51-60 40
    LETTERS 61-70 43
    LETTERS 71-80 47
    LETTERS 81-90 51

ABOUT BOOKCAPS 56

Historical Context

Alice Walker grew up in a small town in Georgia, in the mid-1900's. Her parents were sharecroppers, and she grew up hearing of the struggles and oppression of African-Americans in the sharecropping system. Seeing how black people were treated in the South, Walker threw herself heavily into the civil rights movement.

Although she was privileged to go to good colleges and to travel, she did experience her share of hardships, which probably helped her to write many of her stories. She was shot in the eye, accidentally, by one of her brothers, which caused her to be half blind and often discriminated against throughout her adolescence. Also, she found herself pregnant when she returned from her semester in Uganda as an exchange student and briefly considered suicide before finally deciding to have the baby aborted.

"The Color Purple" is a story about several black women living in the south who are going through various degrees of struggle in their lives. It is probable that Walker drew inspiration from her real life tribulations, her involvement in the civil rights movement and her experience with the injustice faced by sharecroppers.

Though many African American male critics have panned the novel, stating that it paints a negative picture of black men and feeds into stereotypes, black women see it as empowering and inspiring.

Walker has become a favorite author for women all over the world, regardless of race, and one of the most successful and well-known contemporary American authors.

Plot

The story starts with the narrator, a fourteen-year-old girl named Celie, living in the backcountry of Georgia with her sister, Nettie, their dying mother, and their father, Alphonso. Celie is sexually abused by Alphonso and impregnated by him twice. In both cases, Alphonso took the baby from her and got rid of it. Even through the death of Celie's mother, and a new wife, Alphonso continues to abuse her.

Celie's younger and prettier sister, Nettie, is desired by a man known as Mr. _____, who already has a woman in his life; a lounge singer by the name of Shug Avery. Alphonso refuses to allow Nettie to marry Mr. _____, but offers Celie to him and he accepts. Nettie runs away from Alphonso's house and lives with Celie and Mr. _____ for a time, but eventually Nettie runs off, and Celie assumes she has died because she does not hear from her anymore.

Mr. _____'s son, Harpo, impregnates and marries a large woman named Sofia with an exuberant personality. Harpo and Mr. _____ constantly try to berate Sofia, but to no avail because Sofia is both physically and mentally stronger than they are.

When Shug becomes sick, Mr. _____ allows her to stay in his house where Celie develops a sexual attraction to her. Shug stays at the house to save Celie from being beaten my Mr. _____ and the two women soon develop a sexual relationship with one another.

Shug gets married to a man named Grady, yet continues to have sex with Celie. Shug asks Celie about Nettie and Celie tells her that she assumes Nettie is dead because she has not heard from her and Shug tells her that she has seen Mr. _____ hide letters, which turn out to be from Nettie.

Nettie was taken in by missionaries named Samuel and Corrine and was living in Africa with them, and their two adopted children, which coincidentally look like Nettie. It is revealed that the two children are Celie's from when Alphonso impregnated her, and Alphonso is not really their father, but their stepfather.

When Corrine dies Nettie marries Samuel, and they move back to the states where Celie and Nettie are reunited. Most relationships that suffered throughout the novel are repaired as the characters get older and Celie and Nettie become close once again, happier than they have ever been.

Characters

Celie

The narrator of the novel, though rather than telling the story she writes letters. Celie was abused sexually by her stepfather Alphonso, given to a man named Mr. _____ to marry, and is separated from her sister, Nettie, for many years.

Celie has two children with Alphonso: Olivia and Adam, though she does not even know they are alive for many years. She is poor and uneducated and lives through much abuse. She befriends and has an intimate relationship with Shug Avery and becomes a stronger woman who stands up for herself against those who have abused her.

Nettie

Celie's younger sister whom Celie loves very much. Mr. _____ wants to marry Nettie at first, though Alphonso refuses to allow it and he ends up marrying Celie. Nettie runs away to live with Celie and Mr. _____ for a time but when Mr. _____ makes advances toward her she leaves, not to be heard from for many years.

She meets missionaries named Samuel and Corrine and moves with them to Africa. She writes Celie many letters, though Celie never gets them and paints a picture of Africa for the novel. She cares for Samuel's and Corrine's adopted children, Adam and Olivia, later learning that they are Celie's biological children, and marries Samuel when Corrine dies.

Alphonso

The man whom Celie and Nettie believe to be their father for many years ("Pa"), only later learning that he was, in fact, their step-father rather than their biological father. He favored Nettie, the younger, prettier, daughter over Celie, though Celie is the one he sexually abused.

He is the father of Adam and Olivia, with Celie, though he sold them right after Celie gave birth to them. Alphonso never reforms himself into a decent human being, dying an abuser. When he dies, he leaves his house and property to Celie.

Mr. _____

His real name is Albert, though throughout the novel he is referred to as Mr. _____. He is Celie's husband and he abuses her for a very long time. He originally wanted to marry Nettie, but when Alphonso refused he decided to marry Celie instead. Mr. _____ has a son named Harpo, whom he encourages to assert dominance over his wife, Sofia.

He has feelings for Shug, though he is married to Celie and he hides the letters Nettie sends to Celie from African, leading Celie to believe Nettie is dead. Later in life Mr. _____ transforms himself and feels great guilt for the person he was in the past, and he and Celie eventually form a friendship.

Shug Avery

A blues singer who Celie meets through Mr. _____, who is in love with her and has taken her as his mistress. Shug and Celie do not get along at first, though eventually they become best of friends. Shug and Celie develop a strong friendship that turns into an intimate relationship and Shug teaches Celie how to become a self-confident, independent woman.

She makes Celie feel comfortable, and like she is worth something for the first time in her life and Celie has a very strong love for her because of the gentle way in which she helped to come into her own.

Harpo

Harpo is Mr. _____'s son and the husband of Sofia. Mr. _____ often berates Harpo for looking like less of a man when he allows Sofia to speak her mind. He is very atypical in terms of gender stereotypes because he cries, he likes to do housework, he loves his independent wife, and he kisses his children, all of which are things that supposedly make one less manly.

Harpo attempts, at the encouragement of his father, to physically abuse Sofia, but he fails because she is stronger than he is. Eventually, Harpo realizes the error of his ways and reforms himself and repairs his marriage to Sofia.

Sofia

Harpo's independent, outspoken wife. She is a good friend of Celie's and will not allow anyone to assert their dominance over her, especially whites or men. The mayor tries to hire her to be his maid, to which Sofia says, "hell no", and thus she is arrested and forced to do it anyway for a term of twelve years, in lieu of going to jail.

With this punishment, Sofia realizes why people must not resist those in higher position, or try to single-handedly stop racism, because she endures many hardships over those twelve years.

Corrine

One of the missionaries Nettie befriends and moves to Africa with. She is the adoptive mother of Adam and Olivia, Celie's biological children, unbeknownst to anyone. Corrine notices that Nettie resembles her children very much and begins to resent her. She believes that Nettie is having too close a role in their family and thinks that Nettie and Samuel have had an affair. While Corrine, Samuel, Nettie, Adam, and Olivia are still living in Africa, Corrine gets sick and dies. As Corrine expects, Samuel and Nettie get married soon after.

Samuel

The other missionary that Nettie befriends and moves to Africa with. He is married to Corrine at first and later to Nettie. He is the adoptive father of Adam and Olivia, who are Celie's biological children though no one knows that Nettie is actually related to them.

Samuel is a priest and a very strong black man who makes it his mission to lift the spirits of African Americans all over the world. Samuel takes his family and Nettie to Africa to do missionary work and becomes very close with Nettie.

He tells Nettie a story that informs her that Alphonso is not her biological father, but her stepfather. After Corrine's death, Samuel and Nettie marry.

Squeak

Squeak is a woman who becomes Harpo's lover after Sofia has left him. Squeak is mulatto and thus suffers many of the hardships that other blacks do, even though she is half white. Mulattos were in some cases discriminated against worse than blacks because they were the product of a mixed race relationship.

Squeak is abused just as badly as the other women in the story and eventually, like Celie, becomes a stronger woman who stands up for herself. Once asserting her independence, Squeak insists on being called by her real name, Mary Agnes, and decides that she wants to be a singer.

Adam

The biological son of Celie and Alphonso who was sold by Alphonso right after his birth. He was adopted by Samuel and Corrine and eventually cared for by Nettie, who is actually his aunt.

Adam falls in love with an Olinka girl in Africa named Tashi, and they get married. Adam has a great deal of respect for Tashi and considers her his equal, going against the patriarchal ideals of most other men in the novel. Adam's marriage to an African girl connects Africa and America in the novel and in Celie's mind.

Tashi

Tashi is from the Olinka Village in Africa and is married to Adam. Tashi is very tradition and embraces African culture. She is anti-imperialism and colonization. She is very against white power and the dominance and abuse inflicted by white men against African Americans.

She decides to stay true to her African culture, as a means of differentiating herself physically from other cultures, by undergoing facial mutilation and female circumcision. These are common practices in African culture and set them apart from the rest of the world. Adam also undergoes facial mutilation with Tashi.

Olivia

The biological daughter of Celie and Alphonso, the adopted daughter of Corrine and Samuel, and the sister of Adam. When the family moves to Africa, Olivia becomes very close friends with an Olinka girl named Tashi.

Eventually, Tashi marries Olivia's brother Adam and the two become sisters-in-law. Tashi's and Olivia's friendship shows the strength of bonds between women and also shows that though people are of different cultural backgrounds, they can still develop a close tie to one another.

Miss Millie

Miss Millie is the mayor's wife and the reason that Sofia was asked to be their maid. Miss Millie saw how well kept Sofia's children were and wished to have her as her maid.

Miss Millie is very racist and speaks down to people, thinking she is on a high horse. When Sofia says "hell no" to the request to be their maid, Miss Millie has her arrested. Instead of going to jail, Sofia is sentenced to twelve years as Miss Millie's maid.

Eleanor Jane

The daughter of the mayor and Miss Millie. Eleanor Jane feels very close to Sofia and considers her a friend she would like to come to when she needs emotional support, but Sofia finds it hard to be close to Eleanor Jane because she was treated very poorly by the mayor and Miss Millie for the years she worked for them.

Eleanor Jane does not, at first, understand the struggles and abuse that African Americans have faced, but as she gets older realizes the injustice of it. Eleanor Jane cares for Sofia's daughter, Henrietta, as a sort of penance for what Sofia has gone through.

Themes

The Power of Voice

Celie is taught at an early age to keep her mouth shut about the abuse she endures and this becomes something she carries with her. She becomes attracted to people who abuse her, and she never says anything about it to anyone.

When she meets Sofia and Shug, two women who are very open and outspoken, she learns the power of her own voice. The women teach her that she must stand up for herself, or she will always be walked all over. It is not until Celie learns to stand up for herself and use her voice that she finally achieves happiness and respect.

Female Relationships

Female relationships come in several different forms in this novel, but all of them are very important. Without one another, the women would be less powerful, but together they are a very strong unit.

Nettie and Celie are sisters who lose a lot of time together but remain close when they reunite, Shug and Sofia are close friends of Celie, and Shug is quite a bit more than that as they have a sexual relationship. Women often seem to be pitted against one another by the men, but end up becoming tight and prevailing, stronger than ever.

Learning from the Environment

Most people who are abused tend to become abusers, as most people who are abusers were abused at some point in their lives. People become what they know. Harpo was berated by his father for not being a strong enough force against Sofia, thereby letting Sofia have the upper hand, so he became more forceful with her.

Mr. _____ was abused by his father when he was a boy, so he becomes abusive as a man. When Eleanor Jane has her baby, Sofia tells her that when he grows up he will be a racist because he is raised around racist people.

The Influence of Color

In this novel, color greatly influences mood or represents the characters state in life. Characters often comment on the colors they are seeing and the colors that each character notices represent where they are emotionally at that moment.

When Celie and Kate go shopping they notice that all of the dresses are drab colors. When Mr. _____ has a spiritual awakening, of sorts, he pants the rooms in his house white: bright and clean. Celie notes "the color purple" is one of the greatest things God ever created. Color creates, influences, and describes moods, stations in life, and spiritual state of mind in this novel.

Violence

Violence is prevalent throughout the novel but especially against women. The men in "The Color Purple" use violence to assert their dominance over the women physically, sexually, and emotionally.

Celie is sexually and emotionally abused by Alphonso who rapes her then gives away her children and later physically abused by Mr. _____. Sofia is abused by Harpo, at the encouragement of his father, and some may say that Sofia verbally abuses others.

The abuse of many characters begins at a young age so as they get older they are more apt to abuse others, and they do.

Female Dominance

It may not seem as though there is a lot of female dominance in this novel because there is so much abuse, but there is, especially toward the end. Throughout the novel, Shug and Sofia represent strong women who stand up to men regardless of how they will be treated in return.

These women are not afraid to speak their mind and encourage others to do so, as well. Shug encourages Celie to defend herself against Mr. _____ and she does so, eventually changing Mr. _____ to the core. Though the female dominance may be subtle, it is what makes the women come out on top at the end.

Sex

Sex is seen by Celie as a form of violence for most of her life. When she is a young girl she is molested by her stepfather, Alphonso, for years, resulting in two children whom she never meets until she is much older.

When she is married to Mr. _____, sex is loveless and can be violent, as well. She never enjoys sex because she looks at men with fear and disgust, having only negative experiences with them. She does begin to enjoy sex, or even love, until she meets Shug, making her only satisfying sexual relationship one with a woman.

Religion

Celie writes many of her letters to God, showing her faith in religion despite the struggles she has faced, though she does falter at times. As a young girl and young adult, Celie sees God as an old white man.

Throughout her younger years in life, she is abused by men continuously, and she begins to rebel against the image of God because she sees him as a man. As Celie gets older, wiser, and more independent, she sees God as genderless and thinks of God more spiritually, rather than as an individual.

She sees God as someone/thing that focuses on making people happy and allowing them to enjoy life, rather than human.

Love

Love is a complex matter in this novel because the ties of love are very strong, but necessarily in male/female relationships. The familial love between Celie and Nettie is strong, even when they go years without speaking to one another and the love that Celie and Shug share is very strong.

The love in marriages is almost non-existent because men are seen as violent toward, disloyal to, and disrespectful of the women with whom they are married. The women are like sisters to one another in many cases, thus making the bonds of love more familial than marriage-bound.

Race

Race plays an important role in this novel, mostly because of the setting. The story begins in the South prior to the Civil Rights movement, and the characters are poor, under-educated African Americans. Before the Civil Rights movement, blacks had very few rights and were often abused by white people.

Celie was not proud of the fact that she was African American because she did not see anything to be proud of based on the people of her heritage that she was surrounded by. It was not until she became educated people who were actually from Africa that she was truly proud of who she was.

Chapter Summaries

Letters 1-10

The novel is narrated by Celie in terms of letters, though it opens with one of Celie's memories. She is remembering her father, Alphonso, telling her not to speak of the sexual abuse he has inflicted on her.

In letter one, Celie's mom has just had another child and will not have sex with her husband because she has just given birth and this upsets him. He begins to molest Celie to get what he wants, and her mother has no idea, but is happy that he is not bothering her anymore.

Celie's father tells her not to tell anyone but God about the abuse, and so she begins every letter to God. Celie begins to experience symptoms of morning sickness. Letter two, Celie gives birth to a child and her mother, very sick at this point, is curious to know who the father is.

Celie tells her mother that God is the father and when the baby disappears she tells her mother than God has taken it, though it was really Pa who had done so. Celie's mother dies, and Celie gives birth to a second baby.

23

Celie gives birth to her second child in letter three, this time it is a boy, which Pa also takes away. Pa starts to be very mean toward Celie and critical of the way she looks and everything she does so Celie begins to worry that he will start molesting her younger sister Nettie now. Celie vows to do everything she possibly can to protect her little sister.

By letter four, Pa remarries this time with a girl the same age as Celie whom he spends a lot of time having sex with. Nettie is seeing a much older man, only referred to as "Mr. _____", who is a widower with three children, his wife having been murdered.

Celie encourages Nettie to concentrate on school rather than marrying an older man who already has kids. In letter five, Celie changes her mind about Mr. _____ and wants Nettie to marry him, just for the sake of getting away from Pa, because he is becoming more abusive. He gets mad at Celie because he believes that she winked at a boy though Celie tells him that she did no such thing as she is scared of men. At this point, Celie has stopped getting her period all together and will not likely be able to have any more children.

In letter six, Mr. _____ asks Pa if he can marry Nettie, but Pa refuses. He says that Nettie is much too young, and he disapproves of the fact that Mr. _____ has a mistress: Shug Avery. When Celie sees a picture of Shug Avery that Mr. _____ carries in his wallet she becomes obsessed with her because she is very trendy and beautiful.

By letter seven, Pa's new wife is sick, and possibly pregnant, and Celie dresses up nice to keep Pa interested in her rather than Nettie. Both Nettie and Pa's wife finally realize that Pa has been molesting Celie and are sickened.

When Mr. _____ asks for Nettie's hand once again, Pa refuses but offers him Celie. He says that she is ugly, not a virgin, and lies, but she is good as housework, can't have any more kids and he will throw in a cow and some linens, but Mr. _____ does not accept right away.

In letter eight, Nettie and Celie form a plan to run away together when Celie gets to Mr. _____'s house. They study Nettie's schoolbooks to get smart enough to make a plan. When Celie was pregnant, Pa took her out of school even though she was very smart and loved to go because Pa told her that Nettie was the smart one, so Celie did not need school.

Mr. _____ eventually came around to look at Celie again and said he would take her if he could still get the cow, as well. In letter nine, Celie and Mr. _____ get married, and Harpo, the eldest of his four children, tries to kill Celie by throwing a rock at her head. Celie realizes that no one has brushed his children's hair since their mother died when she cannot get the tangles out. Celie says she thinks of Shug Avery when she is having sex with Mr. _____.

In letter ten, Celie sees a child in town that looks just like her and thinks it must be Olivia, the first child she had with Pa. She offers to give the girl and her mother a ride, asking the little girl's name and age, and afterward convinced that the little girl is, in fact, hers. They end up finding the woman's husband and getting a ride with him.

Letters 11-20

In letter eleven, Nettie moves in with Celie and Mr. _____ because Pa will not leave her alone. Her and Celie study to try to run away. Nettie believes that Celie should stand up against the kids, but Celie does not think she has it in her. When Mr. _____ incessantly hits on Nettie, and she refuses, he kicks her out.

Nettie worries for Celie and promises to write, though Celie never gets any letters. In letter twelve, Mr. _____'s sisters, Carrie and Kate, visit. They did not seem fond of his first wife, favorably comparing Celie to her, though they muse that it was not her fault as he was always off with Shug Avery, whom they were sick of hearing about.

Kate visits again and takes Celie to buy new clothes for the first time in her life, and she tells her that she needs to stand up to the kids. Kate even attempts to tell off Harpo but Mr. _____ comes down on her for it, and she leaves, telling Celie that she needs to take care of herself against them.

In letter thirteen, Harpo inquires to his father as to why he beats Celie. Mr. _____ tells him that it is because Celie is his wife and he needs to keep her in line, so he beats her with his belt. Harpo tells Celie that he is in love with a girl from church whom he wants to marry though he has never spoken to her.

In letter fourteen, Celie learns that Shug Avery is coming to town to sing, and Celie is excited to see her, even though her husband wants to have an affair with her. Celie just wants to look at Shug as she has become sort of obsessed with her.

In letter fifteen, Mr. _____ has just returned from spending the entire weekend with Shug, and he is sad and just sits around and smokes. Celie would like to ask Mr. _____ questions about Shug but she does not.

In letter sixteen, we learn that Harpo works very hard so that Mr. _____ does not have to. Mr. _____ does not appreciate Harpo any more than he does Celie. Harpo is still in love with the girl from church.

By letter seventeen Harpo is still in love with the girl, named Sofia Butler, and she is eight months pregnant with his child. Her father does not approve of him because his mother was murdered and his father does not think the child she is carrying is really Harpo's.

When Harpo does not defend Sofia against his father's accusations, she realizes that he is not independent enough to be a father and tells him that she and the baby will be waiting for him when he is ready.

In letter eighteen, Harpo brings Sofia and the baby to live with him, fixing up his father's shed to make them a home. He works very hard and Mr. _____ pays him for his work. Sofia is a very big and strong woman and the two of them are very happy in their marriage, though Mr. _____ is not happy for them.

In letter nineteen, Celie tells of a time when Harpo asked Celie and Mr. _____ how he can get Sofia to follow his orders. Mr. _____ tells Harpo to beat her, as he does to Celie and Celie agrees, though perhaps more out of jealousy than agreement because she thinks they are too happy to worry about following orders.

Harpo appears later with a black eye, claiming he got kicked by a mule, but it is obvious to Celie that Sofia hit him back. In letter twenty, Sofia and Harpo are in a particularly nasty fight where Sofia is hitting Harpo with logs when he tries to beat her. Sofia definitely has the upper hand in the fight.

Letters 21-30

In letter twenty-one, Celie is having trouble sleeping and thinks it is because of the guilt she feels for telling Harpo to beat Sofia. Sofia finds out Celie told him that and is mad at her at first, until she realizes that Celie is jealous of Sofia for being strong enough to fight back.

Celie thinks she has no feelings at all because she never gets mad, she just talks to God. Sofia feels bad for Celie and the two are friends once again and make a quilt. Shug Avery gets sick in letter twenty-two, and it has the whole town talking. Even the priest, who thinks very highly of Celie, thinks that Shug is a tramp and deserves to be sick for stealing men from other women.

Mr. _____ takes Shug in to have Celie care for her, and Sofia and Harpo are saddened for Celie, though Celie is actually very excited. When Shug comes into the house, she is mean to Celie right off the bat, calling her ugly.

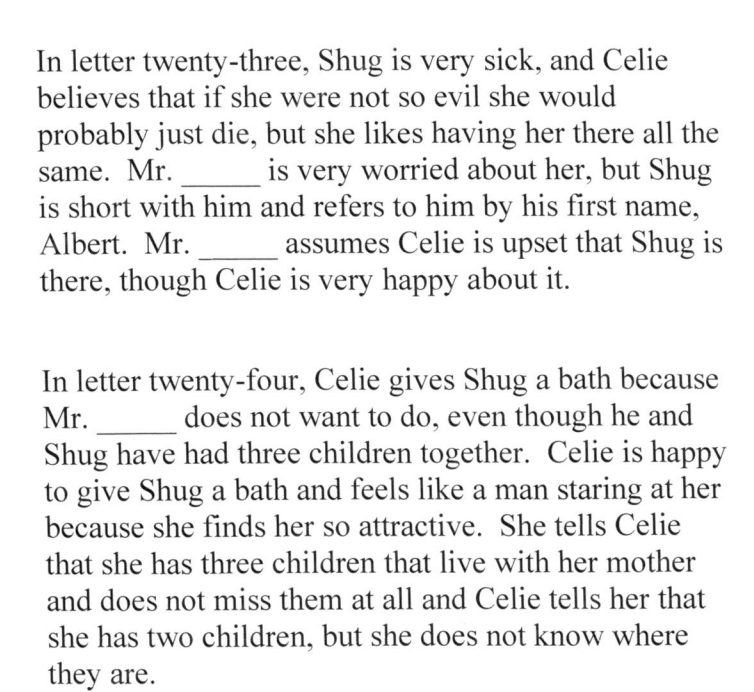

In letter twenty-three, Shug is very sick, and Celie believes that if she were not so evil she would probably just die, but she likes having her there all the same. Mr. _____ is very worried about her, but Shug is short with him and refers to him by his first name, Albert. Mr. _____ assumes Celie is upset that Shug is there, though Celie is very happy about it.

In letter twenty-four, Celie gives Shug a bath because Mr. _____ does not want to do, even though he and Shug have had three children together. Celie is happy to give Shug a bath and feels like a man staring at her because she finds her so attractive. She tells Celie that she has three children that live with her mother and does not miss them at all and Celie tells her that she has two children, but she does not know where they are.

In letter twenty-five, Celie tells of trying to get Shug to eat, though Shug refuses because she is snobby, expecting juice and fruit when Celie is eating ham, biscuits, and gravy. When Celie leaves the room to get Shug some water she returns and sees that Shug ate some of her food and both Celie and Mr. _____ are happy that Shug has finally eaten, Celie getting a sense of satisfaction.

In letter twenty-six, it is obvious that Shug and Celie are getting closer, as Celie gets Shug to sit up in bed and allow her to comb her hair. Shug hums a song that she tells Celie was inspired by her.

In letter twenty-seven, Mr. _____'s father comes to visit, criticizing Mr. _____ for wanting to be with Shug as he finds her trashy. He sympathizes for Celie for her husband's mistress being in their house, but Celie likes Shug and thus spits in Mr. _____'s father's water.

Celie and Mr. _____ both treat Shug with the same revelry, and when Celie attempts (unsuccessfully) to teach Shug to sew she says she feels good and right for the first time in her life.

In letter twenty-eight, Celie and Sofia are working on a quilt together, that contains a piece of Shug's yellow dress and talk about Harpo and his strange new eating habits. He is eating so much food lately that people joke with him that he must be pregnant. In letter twenty-nine, Harpo finally tells Celie that the reason he has been eating so much is because he thinks that if he gets as big as Sofia he may be able to make her mind him.

Celie tells him that she minds his father, but they do not love one another, yet he and Sofia love one another, so they do not need to have control like that in their relationship. She points out that Mr. _____ does love Shug and Shug does not allow him to abuse her. Harpo cries and throws up all of the extra food he ate that day.

In letter thirty, Celie tells Sofia about Harpo's plan to get as big as her and Sofia tells her that she is thinking of leaving him and moving in with her sister and that she does not even want to have sex with him anymore like she used to. Celie thinks that she has never wanted to have sex with Mr. _____, she just lets him do it. The only person she gets excited thinking about is Shug.

Letters 31-40

In letter thirty-one, Sofia makes the decision to leave Harpo and her and the children go to live with her sister. Harpo acts like he does not care at all, and Celie gives Sofia the quilt they made to take with her. In letter thirty-two Harpo realizes that he is good looking and turns the little shed, and he and Sofia had made their home into a dance spot.

Celie asks Harpo what Sofia will think when she comes back, and Harpo tells Celie that Sofia is not going to come back. In letter thirty-three, Harpo starts getting more people coming into his juke joint as Shug begins to sing there.

Celie loves watching Shug sing there, although Mr. _____ does not like her to go because he feels as though his wife shouldn't do such things. Shug sings a song for Celie, and she feels more special than she ever has before.

In letter thirty-four, Shug and Harpo are making a lot of money with Shug singing at Harpo's every weekend. The time comes for Shug to leave and Celie is as sad as she was when Nettie left her.

Celie confides in Shug that Mr. _____ beats her when Shug is not there, so Shug tells Celie she will stay until she is sure that Celie is safe. In letter thirty-five, Celie and Shug have a conversation about sex.

Shug enjoys having sex with Mr. _____ and she does so almost every night, though she does not love him, she just has passion for him. When Celie tells her that she has never in her life enjoyed having sex, Shug proclaims her still a virgin and makes her look at her vagina in the mirror.

Celie tells Shug that she does not mind when Shug has sex with Mr. _____, though that is not true, but not because she is jealous of Shug, more likely because she is jealous of Mr. _____.

In letter thirty-six, Sofia returns and brings her new boyfriend, Buster with her. She tells Celie that she has had another child and then she meets Harpo and his girlfriend, Squeak. Squeak gets jealous when Harpo and Sofia dance together and calls her a bitch, causing Sofia to punch her in the face.

She then takes Buster and leaves. In letter thirty-seven, Celie tells Squeak that the reason Harpo is so upset lately is because Sofia has been arrested. She was asked to be the mayor's maid, to which she replied "hell no" and was slapped by the mayor then beaten nearly lifeless by the police. Celie and Mr. _____ visit with Sofia to clean her up. Celie also tells Squeak that she should ask Harpo to call her by her real name, Mary Agnes.

In letter thirty-eight, Celie, Shug, Mr. _____ and Harpo visit Sofia in prison where they learn she is working in the laundry room and surviving by acting subservient and keeping her mouth shut. Sofia is sentenced to twelve years in prison and her children are looked after by her sister, Odessa, and Squeak.

In letter thirty-nine, everyone tries to think of a way to get Sofia out of prison, and Squeak realizes her uncle is the white warden of the prison. They decide to ask him if there is anything he can do to help Sofia. In letter forty, in an effort to get Sofia out of prison, they dress Squeak up like a white woman and send her to see the warden. She tells the warden that Sofia really loves being in prison, and it is not punishment for her at all, but working for a white family would be the worst punishment she could be given.

Letters 41-50

In letter forty-one, Warden Hodges notices that Squeak is, in fact, a Hodges but does not approve because she is mulatto. Squeak tries to explain to the warden that Sofia is not being punished being forced to do laundry but the warden is only interested in who Squeak's family is.

The warden beats and rapes Squeak, and when she gets home and tells everyone what happens she finally tells Harpo to call her Mary Agnes. In letter forty-two, Mary Agnes decides that she wants to become a singer and starts to sing. Her voice is very high pitched and funny, almost like a cat's meow.

At first everyone makes fun of it, but eventually they start to really enjoy her singing. In letter forty-three Sofia is released from jail and sentenced to twelve years serving the mayor's family. The son is a terror and Celie cannot believe that Sofia has to look after him, but the daughter, Eleanor Jane is very sweet and loves Sofia.

In letter forty-four we learn that Sofia thinks her job with the mayor's family is slavery, though their son tells her she is a captive, not a slave. Miss Millie, the mayor's wife whom Sofia teaches to drive, allows Sofia to return home for Christmas for the first time since she started working for them five years prior.

Sofia only gets to stay with them for fifteen minutes as Miss Millie cannot back out of the driveway and will not allow a black man to drive her home, so Sofia needs to drive her. In letter forty-five Shug comes back to town, bringing with her a surprise that Mr. _____ is going to be a car for him because Shug is making a lot of money now.

Shug does bring a car, but it is one that she bought for herself as a wedding present, because her real surprise is her new husband, a man named Grady. Both Celie and Mr. _____ are devastated by this revelation.

In letter forty-six, Mr. _____ and Grady spend the holidays drinking while Celie and Shug chat and catch up on what they have missed. Shug is famous now and has a lot of money, and she tells Celie that Mr. _____ is only like a family member to her now; she has no romantic feelings for him.

Celie tells Shug that Mr. _____ does not beat her anymore, and he makes an effort to make sex enjoyable for her. She tells Shug that she is still a "virgin" in Shug's eyes though because she has yet to have an orgasm or to enjoy sex at all.

In letter forty-seven, Celie finally tells Shug that her father molested her and her two children resulted from that incestuous relationship though her mother never knew. She tells Shug that no one has ever loved her, and Shug tells her that she loves her then kisses her right on the mouth and again on her breast, to which Celie is happy to reciprocate.

In letter forty-eight, Shug and Celie wake up next to each other, which Celie thinks is the best feeling she has ever had, while the men show up still drunk from the night before. Shug thinks that Mary Agnes should start signing in front of people, suggesting that the two of them sing together at Harpo's one-night but Harpo refuses.

In letter forty-nine, Shug asks Celie about Nettie because Nettie is the only thing Celie ever loved, other than Shug. She tells Celie that she thinks she saw a letter from Nettie one day when Mr. _____ got the mail and thus the women are on a mission to find the hidden letters. In letter fifty, Shug gets close to Mr. _____ again, much to the chagrin of Celie and Grady, but she says it is just, so she can find out where the letters are.

Shug tells Celie all about her life and the reason she was attracted to Mr. _____ and how she can't believe he has changed so much since she first met him.

Letters 51-60

In letter fifty-one, Celie and Shug find that Nettie's letters are locked in Mr. _____'s trunk along with a pair of Shug's underwear and some dirty photos. They decide that rather than take the entire letters, they will leave the envelopes, so he will not notice that they are missing.

In letter fifty-two, Nettie's first letter tells Celie about when she left Albert's house how he followed her and tried to rape her, but she hurt him and got away. Albert told Nettie that she and Celie would never hear from one another again.

Nettie ended up in the house of a missionary minister, and she noticed that his adopted daughter was really Celie's biological daughter, Olivia. In letter fifty-three, Nettie tells Celie of the Minister, Samuel's family, which consists of his wife, Corrine, and their adopted children, Adam and Olivia. They are very welcoming to her and very religious.

In letter fifty-four, Nettie writes her third letter to Celie and realizes that Celie is not getting any of them. She cannot find any work in town and thinks she may have to leave, leaving Celie behind.

Corrine and Samuel will be going to Africa to be missionaries, and Nettie does not want to leave them either. In letter fifty-five, Nettie's fourth letter, she tells Celie that she is in Africa with Olivia and Adam and thinks they are wonderful people. She is learning a lot about African culture and shares her knowledge with Celie. She tells Celie that she is positive now that Adam and Olivia are Celie's kids and tells her that they are being well taken care of.

In letter fifty-six, Nettie writes in her fifth letter to Celie about all of the pride she is developing in being a black person. She always felt her race was a disadvantage, but she is learning of many well-off black people that she never saw growing up, and Samuel tells her that, in Africa, they have an advantage over white people.

Nettie realizes all of the people in the Bible, including Jesus, were black. In letter fifty-seven, Nettie's sixth letter, she tells Celie about Samuel who is the first kind black man she has ever met and how she thinks Corrine is lucky to have him. She tells Celie of all of the places she is travelling to and the nice people she is meeting and fills her in on all of the history she is learning about African Americans and slavery.

In letter fifty-eight, Nettie's seventh letter to Celie, she tells of her first view of Africa and how lucky she felt to be seeing it with her own eyes. She tells Celie that the people in Africa are darker than any she has ever seen, but it is mostly run by white men who speak of the native Africans disparagingly. She notes many similarities between Africa and home.

In letter fifty-nine, Mr. _____ and Grady return and Celie is so mad at Albert for hiding her letters that she wants to kill him, though she listens to Shug when she tells her not to. She asks Shug to convince Albert to allow them to share a bed for the rest of the time she is visiting, and Shug does.

Letter sixty brings a very grievous and angry Celie who sleeps next to Shug but they do not get intimate because of the way Celie is feeling. She has no desire, even for Shug. Shug and Celie buy some fabric to make Celie some pants to make working in the fields easier for her.

Letters 61-70

In letter sixty-one Celie is excited that her sister is still alive and begins to daydream about running off with Nettie and Adam and Olivia. She reads Nettie's next letter where she describes the Olinka Village they visit, where the village people are very surprised that the missionaries are black.

The villagers tell the missionaries about the history of their village and why they worship rootleaf. The villagers point out that the kids look like Nettie rather than Corrine. In letter sixty-two, Nettie tells Celie of Olivia and how smart she is. The Olinka people do not believe in educating females because to them a woman's only job is to marry and have children.

Olivia is the only girl in school, but when she leaves school she teaches everything she learns to her Olinka friend, Tashi. The village women joke with Olivia that she will become the chief's youngest wife, which they think is an honor, but Olivia does not think so. The villagers think that Nettie is Samuel's second wife, and this infuriates Corrine who immediately starts getting jealous.

In letter sixty-three, Nettie tells Celie that Tashi's parents are getting very upset that Tashi shows no interest in learning the women's role in life in the Olinka tribe, because Nettie knows she is learning about the real world from Olivia.

Tashi's parents, especially her father who reminds Nettie of Pa, do not respect Nettie because she is a single, independent woman with different morals than their own, and do not like the missionaries. They do not want Tashi spending time with them, but would like Olivia to come to their place, so they can teach her how to be an Olinka woman.

In letter sixty-four, Nettie tells Celie that she and Corrine are not friends anymore because Corrine thinks that Nettie and Samuel have feelings for one another, especially with Samuel's new interest in the dynamic of polygamous relationships. Tashi's father dies, and her mother now encourages her to get an education outside of the tribe.

In letter sixty-five, Nettie tells Celie that the Olinka Village is being destroyed by an English rubber company that is building a road through town, tearing down their buildings, charging villagers rent, and tax their water.

As Corrine gets very sick with a fever, women of the Olinka tribe begin to encourage their daughters to get an education. In letter sixty-six, Nettie tells Celie that Corrine is very sick still and has taken to resenting Nettie more than ever, believing that Adam and Olivia are Nettie and Samuel's children from before Corrine came along. She makes them both swear this is not the case and examines Nettie's body to see if it looks like she has given birth before.

Corrine resents her children and treats them poorly, which they do not understand as they are not aware they are adopted. In letter sixty-seven, Nettie tells Celie of how she learned the truth about their Pa and the children from Samuel.

Samuel tells them that he got the children from Pa, whom he knew before he became religious and that he was their stepfather and their real father had been lynched by white men. Samuel believed when he met Nettie that he was the children's birth mother, which is why he took her in.

In letter sixty-eight, Celie is completely flabbergasted, and her world is turned around with this new information from Nettie. All these years she believed her children were incest, but it turns out that the man she believed to be her father was not.

Shug tells Celie that the two of them are going to move to Tennessee together. In letter sixty-nine Celie writes to Nettie, instead of God, for the first time as she will continue to do. She tells Nettie that she and Shug went to visit Pa and she told him that she knows the truth.

Pa has a new fifteen-year-old wife who thinks he is wonderful, and no children as his second wife ran off with them. Celie looks for her parent's graves, cannot find them, and decides that Shug is her family now.

In letter seventy, Nettie tells Celie that Corrine is dying. Nettie tells Corrine the truth about the children, but she still believes that Nettie and Samuel are lying to her.

Letters 71-80

In letter seventy-one, Nettie tells Celie that she tries very hard to get Corrine to remember the time, man years ago, when Celie ran into Corrine and Olivia in a fabric store. Corrine does not remember so Nettie brings out a quilt and asks Corrine if she remembers where she got the fabric.

Corrine finally remembers, thinking Olivia and Celie had looked so much alike she wanted to forget about her as quickly as possible before she tried to take Olivia back. As Corrine is dying, she tells Samuel that she believes him and Nettie, finally.

In letter seventy-two, Nettie tells Celie that Olivia has gotten her period, and they buried Corrine in the traditional Olinka manner. Samuel gives Nettie Corrine's old clothing because she is in need of new clothing and he asks her to tell him about Celie.

In letter seventy-three, Celie tells Nettie about her and Shug's talks about God. Celie feels like God has given her a raw deal in life and sees him as an old white man. Shug tells her that God is gender-less and can be found inside each person, rather than in a church, and God gives people things to make them happy in the midst of struggle, like "the color purple".

Celie feels slightly foolish for being so bitter and tries to see life with more positive eyes. In letter seventy-four, Sofia finally returns home after working for the mayor for over eleven years, and feels like there is no place for her in her family because her kids do not really remember her and Harpo has been in a relationship with Mary Agnes for as long as Sofia has been gone.

Shug tells everyone that she, Grady, and Celie will be moving to Tennessee and Mr. _____ cannot believe his ears. Celie unleashes on him and tells him what she really thinks of him for abusing her and keeping Nettie from her.

The women all begin to laugh at the men who do not understand what is happening as secrets are thrown around and Mary Agnes decides to go to Tennessee as well to become a singer. Sofia agrees to look after her child and take care of Harpo.

In letter seventy-five, Mr. _____ tells Celie that Shug is pretty and that is why people like her and Celie is not. Celie confronts Mr. _____ about hiding her letters, and he is shocked. She curses at him numerous times, tells him that she will not speak to him again until he changes his ways, and she, Shug, Grady, and Mary Agnes leave for Memphis.

In letter seventy-six, Celie gets to Shug's house and comments on how lovely and rich it is. When Shug goes on the road to sing, Celie begins making pants for everyone she knows, and it becomes her passion and her business. She makes a pair to send to Nettie in Africa.

In letter seventy-seven, Celie proclaims that she is finally happy for the first time in her life. Her pants business is doing so well that she has hired twins named Darlene and Jerene to work with her.

Darlene tries to teach Celie to speak properly because she thinks Shug will be more proud of her if she does, but Shug says she does not care how Celie speaks, she could speak sign language, and it would be okay.

In letter seventy-eight, Celie tells of her visit back home where people do not recognize her because she has changed so much. She introduces Sofia and Harpo to weed, which Grady grows and sells and Mary Agnes has become quite fond of.

They all get stoned together. Celie sees Mr. _____ at Sofia's mother's funeral and is informed by Sofia that he has changed quite a bit. He does housework now and has become much kinder. Sofia says he almost died from being sick with guilt about what he did to Celie, but he got better when he sent Celie the rest of Nettie's letters.

Celie has a conversation with Mr. _____ and is surprised at how kind he is to her. In letter eighty, Nettie tells Celie that she and Samuel have married, and, with the kids, they are leaving Africa, having felt as though they failed the Olinka's because the village is basically depleted.

Adam is sad, and they learn that it is because he is worried about Tashi who has been left behind and plans to go through the traditional African mutilation and female circumcision. Nettie decides to tell Adam and Olivia about Celie.

Letters 81-90

In letter eighty-one, Nettie tells Celie that they returned to the Olinka village to let them know that the missionary society they visited in England would not help the Olinka's, which the villagers are disappointed about.

They learn that while they were gone Tashi had undergone her mutilations, and they know that Adam will be very upset about it. Tashi is ashamed at the scars on her face, but she knows that her village is proud of her for following tradition in an effort to keep their culture going.

Adam really wants to return to America, but Nettie and Samuel are very happy with their marriage and life at this point. In letter eighty-two, Celie informs Nettie that Alphonso ("Pa") died in his sleep.

Daisy, Pa's widow, tells Celie that her and Nettie own Pa's house and store because they had actually belonged to their birth father, but they were never informed of this before. At first Celie does not want anything he has left her but Shug convinces her to take the stuff and sell her pants in the store.

Celie finds that the house she is inheriting is a nice new house, rather than the one she grew up in and is happy to have a place to call home for herself and Nettie's family when they return.

In letter eighty-three, Celie goes back to Nashville and Shug tells her that she is leaving her for a nineteen year old boy who plays in her backup band and goes into way too much detail about him. She realizes Celie is hurting, and she cries.

Shug does not understand why she is jealous now but was never jealous of Grady (who is now running a weed plantation in Panama with Mary Agnes), and Celie tells her it is because Grady was dull. Celie is heartbroken and stops speaking, instead writing down her answers to Shug's questions.

Shug does not understand why Celie is so upset and Celie decides that although she loves Shug she cannot stay at her home anymore. In letter eighty-four, Henrietta, the youngest child of Sofia's, is very sick with a blood disease and everyone tries to treat it with yams, which they mix in to everything she eats although she hates them.

Mr. _____ is becoming very sensitive and collects seashells. He asks Celie the first question he has ever asked her about herself, if there is anything she likes the way he likes seashells. She tells him that she likes birds. He apologizes for the way he treated her, and she cries. She tells him that men are all the same to her, they are all frogs no matter how you kiss them.

In letter eighty-five, Celie finds out via telegram that Nettie and Samuel were on a boat that sunk on its way to America. Celie gets all of the letters back that she had sent to Nettie and begins to be very depressed about losing her sister, after thinking she had finally gotten her back.

Letter eighty-six is from Nettie, telling Celie that Adam and Olivia are very upset to have lost their friend, Tashi, who has joined the mbeles tribe with her mother. Apparently, anyone who joins the mbeles tribe never comes back alive.

Nettie comments that is has been thirty years since she and her sister have shared a word between them. She worries about how Celie has held up with Mr. _____ and how the children will adapt to life back in America. She says that Adam has gone after Tashi.

Letter eighty-seven is Celie worrying about her own image, feeling uncomfortable in her own skin and musing over why Shug does not want her. Celie and Mr. _____ bond over Shug leaving because he knows what it feels like.

Eleanor Jane, the mayor's daughter who is fond of Sofia, visits Sofia with her new husband and new baby and is upset when Sofia refuses to say nice things about the baby. Sofia explains to Eleanor Jane that she was treated very poorly by her family and will never respect a white person.

Mr. _____ begins to ask Celie many things about her life, and her children and they become friends. Celie continues to get letters from Nettie, even after she has died.

In letter eighty-eight, Nettie tells Celie that Adam and Tashi returned together and were fighting because Adam wants to marry her and she does not want to marry him. She believes that once they get to the U.S. he will fall for a woman with lighter skin.

Adam goes through the same scarring ritual that Tashi went through and honored by his commitment she agrees to marry him. They then set out for America. In letter eighty-nine, Shug tries to help Celie to find out about Nettie's boat, but they can find nothing.

55

Eleanor Jane found out the story about how Sofia began working for them and felt terrible, forming a new friendship with Sofia. Celie and Mr. _____ have deep discussions about the meaning of life, and it is obvious that he is a changed man.

Shug finally returns to Celie, where she has her own bedroom, having left her young boyfriend, and she is jealous of what Albert and Celie may have been doing in her absence. Letter ninety, the final letter, is addressed to God thanking him for bringing Nettie back to Celie. She and Mr. _____ were sitting on the porch one day and saw a family get out of a car, and she realized it was her sister whom she had not seen in many years.

They have a family reunion, even being joined by Mary Agnes who has left Grady, and they comment on how old they all have gotten. Celie believes this is the youngest any of them has ever felt.

About BookCaps

We all need refreshers every now and then. Whether you are a student trying to cram for that big final, or someone just trying to understand a book more, BookCaps can help. We are a small, but growing company, and are adding titles every month.

Visit www.bookcaps.com to see more of our books. Or contact us with any questions.

Printed in Germany
by Amazon Distribution
GmbH, Leipzig